Margaret's Night in ST. PETER'S

*The story of a stray that was born
on the Via della Conciliazione in Rome
and is adopted by the Pope, and how she then runs the
Vatican from museum to floorboard. For ages six and up.*

A NEW SERIES

This volume was preceded by
The Pope's Cat

Margaret's Night in ST. PETER'S

(A Christmas Story)

JON M. SWEENEY

Illustrated by ROY DELEON

PARACLETE PRESS

BREWSTER, MASSACHUSETTS

Λ   Λ

2018 First Printing

Margaret's Night in St. Peter's

(A Christmas Story)

Text copyright © 2018 by Jon M. Sweeney
Illustrations copyright © 2018
by Roy DeLeon

ISBN 978-1-61261-936-1

Library of Congress Cataloging-in-Publication Data
Names: Sweeney, Jon M., 1967- author. | DeLeon, Roy, illustrator.
Title: Margaret's night in St. Peter's (a Christmas story) / Jon M. Sweeney ;
illustrated by Roy DeLeon.
Description: Brewster, Massachusetts : Paraclete Press, [2018] | Series:
The Pope›s cat ; 2 | Summary: Margaret, the Pope›s cat, is bothered by unusual
activity in the Vatican but relaxes in the presence of Michelangelo›s Pietá
before attending Midnight Mass in St. Peter›s Basilica.
Identifiers: LCCN 2018017023 | ISBN 9781612619361 (paperback)
Subjects: | CYAC: Cats—Fiction. | Popes—Fiction. | Catholics—Fiction.
| Christian life—Fiction. | Christmas—Fiction. | Vatican City—Fiction. |
BISAC: RELIGION / Christian Education / Children & Youth. | JUVENILE
FICTION / Holidays & Celebrations / Christmas & Advent. | JUVENILE
FICTION / Religious / Christian / Animals. | JUVENILE FICTION / Religious
/Christian / Holidays & Celebrations. | JUVENILE FICTION / Religious /
Classification: LCC PZ7.1.S9269 Mar 2018 | DDC [E]—dc23
LC record available at https://lccn.loc.gov/2018017023

Published by Paraclete Press
Brewster, Massachusetts
www. paracletepress.com
Printed in the United States of America

*This one is for Spike, Cleo, Cortez, Bowie,
Katana, and Mia.*
—Jon

*For my forever Christmas gifts,
Annie, Xenia, and Marita*
—Roy

CHAPTER 1

*B*ang! *Slam! Boom!* Loud sounds in St. Peter's Square had been going on for nearly an hour already. Margaret was annoyed, because as you may know, cats like to sleep. A lot.

The apartment where Margaret lives with the Pope, ever since he adopted her off the streets of Rome, looks out onto St. Peter's Square. And the noises down there kept waking Margaret up.

She rolled over, covering her ears with her paws.

A few minutes later, the sounds began again, as more trucks arrived to unload even more chairs. *Beep, beep, beep, beep* went the trucks as they backed up to where men in yellow jackets were waiting to unload them. Then came *Bang! Slam! Boom!* all over again, as the men arranged the chairs in rows facing the portico of St. Peter's Basilica.

All of this was in preparation for a special event to take place the following day, Christmas.

Margaret understood a few things about the special occasion being planned for tomorrow because she had heard the Pope and his secretary, Father Felipe, talking about it.

She knew that it was going to be Christmas.

She knew that Christmas in the Vatican was always beautiful.

And she knew that many thousands of people would be coming to celebrate Christmas there with them.

But she still wasn't quite awake.

Margaret snuggled into the couch cushion once more, rolling over just slightly. However, at just the moment when she was again perfectly snug, down in the Square someone turned on a sound system and the Christmas carol "O Come, All Ye Faithful" began to play from a large pair of speakers.

Margaret finally gave up.

She stood on her pillow and stretched—the way that only cats can stretch, as if it is the most strenuous thing they have done for months. And then she got up.

It was almost noon.

The door to the papal apartments opened and in walked Father Felipe. The Pope was standing across the room from Margaret's couch, near a window. He was looking down into St. Peter's Square at all that was going on.

"Eighty thousand people?" the Pope said, turning to Felipe, as if he still couldn't believe something Felipe had said earlier.

Then, the Pope added, "Is that how many people they say will be here tomorrow?"

"Yes, Holy Father," Felipe replied.

"How can they possibly fit?" said the Pope, still looking out the window.

"They always do, Holy Father. Even if they must stand, or sit on someone's shoulders, they will squeeze themselves in for such a special papal blessing."

The Pope then turned and saw that Margaret was awake.

"Ah! Mia dolce Margaret," he said, reaching down to pick her up from the couch. *Mia dolce* means "my sweet" in Italian. And holding her close to his face, the Pope touched his forehead to hers. Margaret purrrrrrrred.

Father Felipe interrupted them. "Your Holiness," he said, "we are late for your audience with the Princess of Sweden. The Swedish children's choir has been practicing for nearly an hour."

"What do you say, *mia dolce?*" the Pope said to Margaret, picking her up and tucking her into his cassock. "Should we go?" Margaret purred again, peeked out, and smiled at Felipe.

Felipe grimaced, but only slightly.

A moment later, the three of them were in the corridor on their way to see the Princess and the children.

The children's choir sang beautifully—that is, when the boys and girls were not *giggling* at Margaret, who kept poking her head in and out of the Pope's robe as if she were playing peek-a-boo.

She wasn't trying to play a game, or make the children laugh. She was simply shy, and unsure whether or not she was supposed to come out and play.

"A-hem!" said the choir director, at one point, when the *giggling* began. "Pay attention, please, children!"

"It is okay," the Pope said, putting his palms together in front of him, looking at the director and then the children.

"Please, please sing, and don't mind Margaret. She is enjoying the children, and the children are enjoying her."

"Besides," the Pope added, "laughing is good for the soul!"

Then, everyone laughed for a moment, even the choir director.

The children sang three songs all together, and the last one was in Swedish. Margaret didn't understand any of the songs, but she enjoyed the singing very much.

When the concert was over, the Pope needed to talk with the Princess of Sweden, so Felipe agreed to take Margaret back home. They walked together down the long corridor, past the Swiss Guard men, and into the Pope's apartment.

CHAPTER 2

Margaret ate her lunch while the Pope was away. A Swiss Guard knocked gently on the door, then opened it, and set down a tray on the coffee table. He smiled at Margaret, but didn't say a thing.

On the tray was a large plate of *Insalata di granchio*—that's crab salad, Margaret's new favorite dish.

An hour later, she was licking her face clean of creamy dressing and crab when she heard people talking and laughing below her window. Margaret jumped up onto the table and looked down into St. Peter's Square.

Tourists in the Square had become accustomed to seeing Margaret in the Pope's apartment windows. This is why, when she jumped up onto the table, she quickly heard cheers as her nose pressed against the window. Looking down, she saw people waving excitedly up at her.

It was Christmas Eve, and crisp and cold in Rome, even for late December. At two o'clock in the afternoon, those rows of chairs in the Square were still empty. Margaret could see all the way down the Via della Conciliazione, where she used to live.

She saw a young man holding yellow balloons. She saw a group of Capuchin friars sitting at a table, having lunch. And there were children in school uniforms singing. Just then, Margaret glimpsed a group of nuns holding a placard with a blown-up photograph of a cat on it—looking just like Margaret—smiling as they looked up at her in the window!

Margaret sniffed, turned away, and jumped down.

The Pope was not yet back from his audience with the Princess. Margaret was bored. She wanted to play with someone or something. A tiny stuffed mouse seemed interesting for a few seconds—with one paw Margaret flipped it into the air—but it fell behind a couch. So, she went to the closed door that led into the corridor and stuck one of her paws underneath it, as if she was searching for something on the other side.

At that moment, to Margaret's great surprise, the door of the apartment quietly opened—it must not have been firmly closed—revealing an empty corridor.

As Margaret emerged from the apartment, she saw a Swiss Guard returning to his post in the hall, and she paused. But he simply gave her a wink.

Then, she heard something. The carpets are thick and the floors don't creak, but Margaret could hear the Pope coming, because cats—as you may know—hear better than human beings do. She jumped back.

"*Mia cara, piccola,*" said the Pope with a grin, as he rounded the corner. In Italian, that means, "My darling, little one." The Pope bent down and picked her up. Margaret purrrrrred.

"Where are you going?" the Pope asked her. And then, "Should we go together? Yes, of course we should," he added, answering his own question.

Father Felipe was there, too. He interjected, "Holy Father, please don't forget that we still have to discuss the final details for tonight."

"Yes, of course," the Pope replied, adding, "we have plenty of time, Father."

What was happening tonight? Margaret wondered.

But then, picking up Margaret in both arms, the Pope said, "Let's go say hello to St. Peter!" And they were off.

Now, the Pope cannot easily go for a walk, visit a museum, or even stroll through his own church without being accompanied by secretaries or members of the Roman Curia. The Curia are the hundreds of Vatican officials who assist popes in their work. And so, by the time Margaret and the Pope reached St. Peter's Basilica a few minutes later, they had two secretaries and one scheduler following close at their heels.

Each of these assistants to the Pope was trying to ask him questions about something they thought he might want to attend to.

"We'll see you in an hour," the Pope finally said with a smile, as they entered the nave of the great church.

The Curia stopped in their tracks as the Pope and Margaret then crossed a threshold into the Basilica and the Pope reached for holy water from a basin that had cherubs on either side. The Pope crossed himself, and then he touched Margaret between the eyes with his still-damp fingers.

The nave of a basilica is its largest, central aisle. A nave is big like a ship, and this one was bigger than any building, church or otherwise, that Margaret or anyone else had ever set eyes on.

"St. Peter's church," the Pope said, and then added, "He was buried right here," pointing to the floor under their feet.

As the Pope and Margaret walked into the nave, tourists took pictures of them, and other people bowed as they walked by. The Pope smiled at everyone, and using the hand not holding Margaret, he touched the heads of some children who rushed up to say hello. Then, a teenage girl even took a selfie with the Pope and his cat.

As Margaret and the Pope walked through St. Peter's Basilica, they passed a tall statue of a saint with a spear in his hand. Margaret wasn't afraid when she saw it, because she knew it was just a statue.

"St. Longinus," said the Pope. "And here," he said, placing his hand on the right foot of the next statue they came upon, "is St. Peter."

"As you can see, Margaret, in St. Peter's hands are the keys of heaven," the Pope said.

"Put your paw here, Margaret, on top of mine," said the Pope.

She did.

"This is how we ask St. Peter for help, as pilgrims have done for centuries."

And together, the Pope and Margaret touched his foot and looked up at St. Peter's serene face, his eyes closed in prayer.

But the moment lasted only a few seconds—because then, the secretaries came rushing up to them again and began to talk about concerns they had regarding plans for that evening. Margaret couldn't understand all of what they were saying, but it had something to do with photographers and reporters.

Then, Father Felipe appeared, too. He ran up and blurted, "Holy Father! We need to confirm many details for tonight. Could you come with me, Your Holiness?"

And the Pope, not wanting to disappoint his hard-working secretaries, and sensing Felipe's anxiety, agreed to go. But what about Margaret? Seeing one of his cardinals nearby, an old friend who had just finished saying mass, the Pope said to the cardinal, "Would you mind taking Margaret back to my apartment for me?"

The cardinal nodded, *"Sì, certo."* "Yes, of course," that means.

Then suddenly, the Pope was gone.

CHAPTER 3

Margaret looked around her. She saw dozens, maybe hundreds, of people, but she knew none of them. She was scared. Suddenly, she felt the way that she used to feel when she was on the streets of Rome, before she was adopted by the Pope.

The Pope's friend, the cardinal, was already talking with someone else.

Margaret wanted to run.

But the exits were

a

long

way

away . . . .

If she had looked up—cats, you see, almost never look up—the height of the ceiling would have made Margaret feel dizzy.

There she was, all alone in the middle of the largest church in the world.

Just as she saw the cardinal turning toward her, she ran in the other direction.

No one seemed to notice her.

Looking again toward an exit, she began to run in that direction, because she saw a faint beam of sunlight coming from an open door.

But when she arrived near the exit, a line of tourists and pilgrims was standing there, waiting to come in. Her way of escape seemed to be blocked.

So, Margaret dashed under the feet of two guards, past the ropes that protect a particularly large sculpture in the first chapel of the north aisle of St. Peter's Basilica.

"And here is Michelangelo's famous Pietà," she heard a tour guide, at that moment, say.

Pietà. That's a funny word, Margaret thought to herself.

She poked her head out from behind the sculpture for just a moment, in order to get a good look at it.

She saw a mother holding her dead son.

"The greatest artist of his time, Michelangelo lived and worked in Rome at the end of the fifteenth century and the beginning of the sixteenth century, during the era we now call the Renaissance," the tour guide went on.

"Michelangelo also painted the ceiling of the Sistine Chapel, which we will see later on our tour," she said.

Just then, a boy in the tour group saw Margaret as she poked her head out from behind the sculpture. He squealed with delight and began to point in her direction, but the boy's mother said, "Shhhh, honey. Listen!"

The tour guide went on.

"This marble sculpture is Michelangelo's most famous one. It depicts what is called Pietà, a word that means 'pity,' because it depicts a common but sad

scene from the Passion of Jesus Christ, when, after he was crucified on the cross, his mother, the Virgin Mary, holds him in her arms."

Suddenly, Margaret felt comforted, being so close to such a loving mother. She missed the Pope, and could no longer even remember where he had gone, or why he left, but her anxiety and fear began to fade away.

A moment later and she began to settle down to rest.

CHAPTER 4

There Margaret sat, behind Michelangelo's Pietà in St. Peter's Basilica, for what seemed like hours.

First, she cleaned herself, licking her hands and legs, her back, and then her hands again. Then, she turned around and around in circles, and around,

until she felt comfortable,
settling down
into a ball,
as cats do.

No one could see her, where she lay down behind the sculpture. But she was able to watch the people as they walked by.

Slowly, she began to feel sleepy, despite the noise of the tourists and pilgrims coming and going, taking pictures and talking.

There were more tour guides, too. People were talking in all sorts of languages. It seemed that people visit St. Peter's Basilica from all over the world. And Margaret had even met St. Peter himself!

"Silenzio. Silenzio," Margaret heard again and again.

A nice man, whose job it seemed to be to stand near the Pietà, said that word every minute or so, when the tourists were talking or laughing too loudly. *Silenzio* means "Quiet, please."

Margaret liked that man. She wanted to sleep, and just wait where she was for the Pope to come back.

She did, eventually, fall fast asleep. And when she woke a few hours later it was to the sound of people being asked to quietly— *"Silenzio,"* once again— exit the Basilica. It was dark outside.

What was going on? Margaret was confused. Why were people leaving? She didn't want to leave that place before the Pope came back and found her.

While tourists walked past where Margaret still lay in hiding, out the front doors into the night, Margaret heard many other people moving in the opposite direction, toward the high altar of the Basilica, near where she had been earlier that day.

They were singing.

An organ was playing the same song that Margaret had heard earlier in the day from those loudspeakers in St. Peter's Square. But this time, she heard a choir singing the words . . .

> O come, all ye faithful,
> Joyful and triumphant,
> O come ye, O come ye to Bethlehem.
> Come and behold him,
> Born the king of angels.
> O come let us adore him,
> O come let us adore him . . .

She loved the singing, and now she felt like she knew the song.

Margaret began to purr as she slowly emerged from her hiding place. Then, she began to walk in the direction of the music.

A few people noticed her this time, but they were also busy, hurrying to get to the place where the music was playing.

Near the center of the Basilica, there were people everywhere, mostly sitting in chairs, but many others were looking for somewhere to sit. The whole church seemed to be bathed in a candlelit glow.

Margaret was no longer afraid.

"Midnight Mass is about to begin!" she heard a parent say to her daughter, as the two of them hurried to find a seat in one of the last rows.

Suddenly, Margaret thought to herself, *The Pope must be here!*

She stood up on her hind legs so that she could better see what was happening.

Then, she realized, *So, this is what is happening tonight.* This is what all those secretaries, the Pope, and Father Felipe were preparing for.

As Margaret walked toward the center of the Basilica she smiled as she saw all the children who were there with their parents.

She saw the nuns who had waved to her at the window earlier that morning from down in the Square. They waved to her again.

Margaret felt warm inside, and happy to be there.

Then, Margaret saw the Pope. He was actually walking in her direction, surrounded by many other priests and bishops and cardinals carrying candles and books and other things. The Pope was carrying what looked like a baby in his arms.

Perhaps that is the baby they are singing about in the Christmas carol, Margaret thought to herself.

As the Pope came closer to where she was, Margaret saw that it was not an actual baby, but a doll that he was carrying while everyone sang.

"He is carrying the baby Jesus," Margaret heard a father explain to his son.

"That is who we are singing about," the father said. "Jesus is about to be born in a manger on Christmas Day."

The Pope winked at Margaret when he saw her standing there.

She smiled back at him, and somehow she knew that she shouldn't run up and jump into his arms, even though that is exactly what she wanted to do at that moment.

Instead, she sat down beside a family at the end of one of the long rows of chairs. When she looked to her side, she realized that there beside her was the boy who had been shushed earlier by his mother. They smiled at each other.

The Pope went on to say Mass from the high altar, and Margaret looked at all the people who were listening to him. Most of them, too, were smiling. The whole Basilica seemed to glow with love on Christmas Eve.

Margaret decided that she liked Midnight Mass very much. And she couldn't imagine feeling scared or lonely anymore.

CHAPTER 5

The following day, it was nearly noon, and Margaret was tucking herself inside the Pope's cassock once again. They were in their apartment and preparing to go outside, but not onto the Via della Conciliazione. Not this time.

"This is a big day, Margaret," the Pope said.

"Oh, and I promise not to leave your side today. No one is getting lost today!" he added playfully.

Margaret purrrrrrred.

Also, this time, it was the Pope who seemed to be in a hurry, rather than being hurried by Father Felipe and the others.

"I have so much that I want to say to people," the Pope was saying.

And, "We must get going. I don't want to make everyone wait for me."

"*Urbi et orbi,*" said the Pope, as they walked down the corridor, outside their apartment.

By now, there were a few secretaries running beside them. Father Felipe was there, too. He was carrying a folder of papers. They all looked very serious, but they were excited for what was to come.

The Pope stroked Margaret behind her ears and down her back. "*Urbi et orbi* means, 'to the City and to the World,' my dear," he said.

"This is my opportunity to speak to the people of Rome and to the people of the world about what I think is most important of all."

This made Margaret nervous. *To the world?* she thought to herself.

Then, as they walked outside, she immediately saw the television cameras—rows and rows of cameras— and the photographers and then the eighty thousand people that Father Felipe had predicted.

There stood the Pope with little Margaret tucked in his cassock, on the portico of St. Peter's Basilica, looking out at all those people crammed into St. Peter's Square.

Suddenly, Margaret felt hungry.

What will we be eating for lunch? she thought to herself. She began to dream of fish, clams, crab, spaghetti! Then, *Not now!* she reminded herself.

There would be plenty of time later for eating.

The Pope moved toward the microphone that was set up for him on the portico. Two of the Swiss Guard men were standing close by. One of them winked at Margaret when he saw her peeking out.

She tried to wink back, but as you probably know, cats can't wink very well, so it looked kind of funny. The Swiss Guard smiled, but then he quickly looked serious once again.

Then Margaret tucked herself back inside the Pope's cassock, and like the eighty thousand others who were there, she was very curious to hear what the Pope would say.

THE END